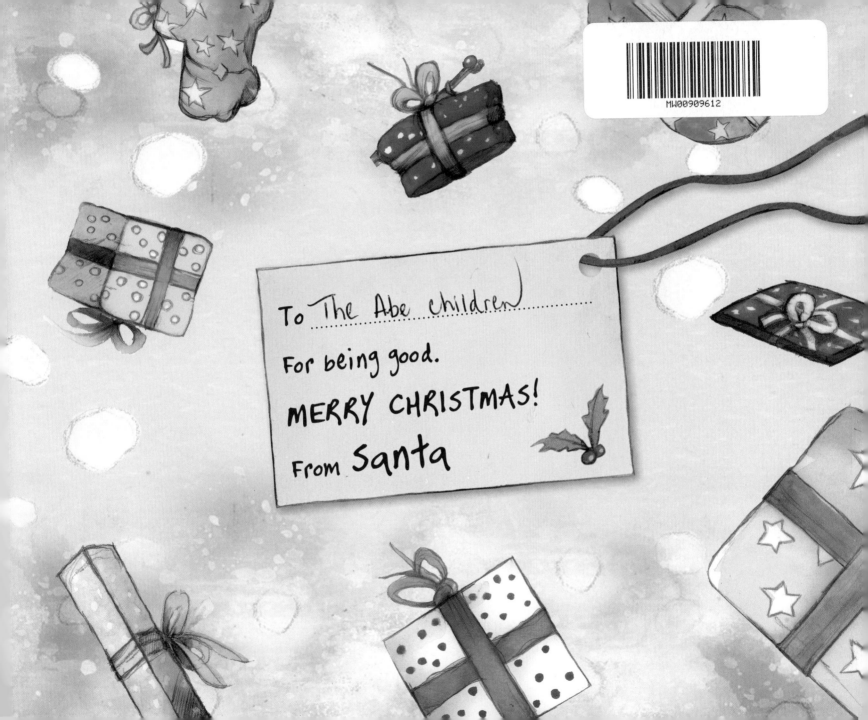

To The Abe children

For being good.

MERRY CHRISTMAS!

From Santa

MW00909612

Santa is coming to Hawaii

Written by Steve Smallman
Illustrated by Robert Dunn and Jerry Pyke
Designed by Sarah Allen

Published by Sourcebooks Jabberwocky, an imprint of Sourcebooks, Inc.
P.O. Box 4410, Naperville, Illinois 60567-4410
(630) 961-3900
Fax: (630) 961-2168
www.jabberwockykids.com

Library of Congress Cataloging-in-Publication data is on file with the publisher.

Source of Production: Leo Paper Products, Guangdong Province, China
Date of Production: May 2015
Run Number: HTW_PO100315
Printed and bound in China
LEO 10 9 8 7 6 5 4 3

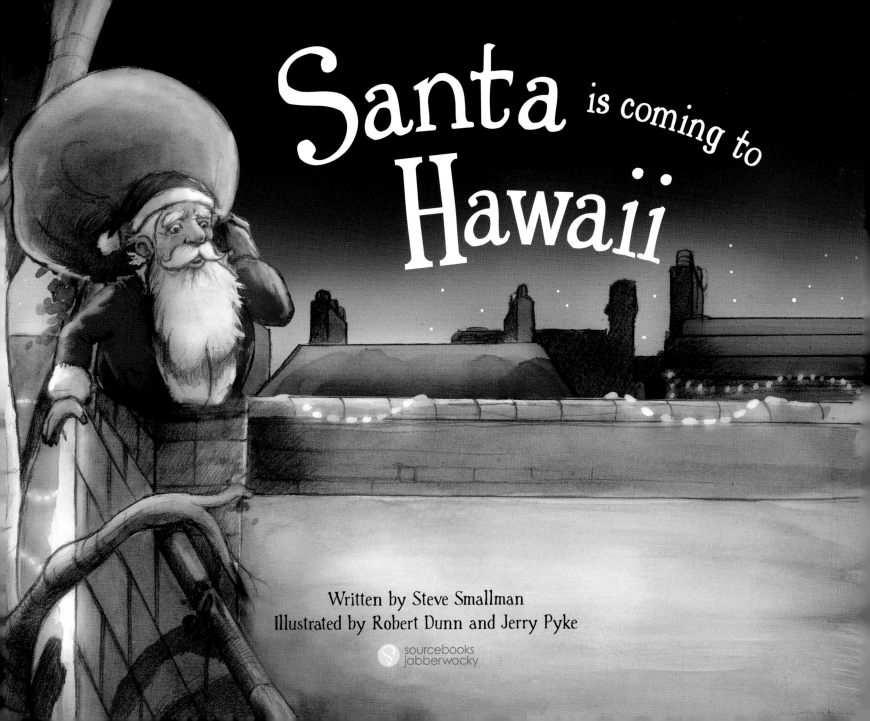

Santa is coming to Hawaii

Written by Steve Smallman
Illustrated by Robert Dunn and Jerry Pyke

sourcebooks
jabberwocky

"Well?"

boomed Santa. "Have all the children from **Hawaii** been good this year?"

"Well...uh...mostly," answered the little old elf, as he bustled across the busy workshop to Santa's desk.

Santa peered down at the elf from behind the tall, teetering piles of letters that the children of Hawaii had sent him.

"Mostly?" asked Santa, looking over the top of his glasses.

"Yes...but they've all been **especially** good in the last few days!" said the elf.

"Jolly good!" chuckled Santa,
"Then we'd better get their presents loaded up!"

Even though the sack of presents was

really, really big

and the elves were **really, really** small,

they seemed to have no trouble loading it onto Santa's sleigh.
Though how they managed to fit such a big sack into one little sleigh
even they didn't know. But somehow they did.

"Splendid!" boomed Santa. "We're ready to go!"

"Er...not quite, Santa," said the little old elf. "One of our reindeer is missing!"

"Missing?

Which reindeer is missing?" asked Santa.

"The youngest one, Santa," said the elf. "It's his first flight tonight. I've called him and called him, but..."

Just then, a young reindeer strolled up, munching on a large carrot.

"Where have you been?"

asked Santa.

But the youngest reindeer was crunching so loudly that it was no wonder he hadn't heard the little old elf calling.

"Oh well, never mind," said Santa, giving the reindeer a little wink. He took out his Santa-nav and tapped in the coordinates for Hawaii. **"This will guide us to Hawaii in no time."**

Crunch!
Crunch!
Crunch!

With a flick of the reins and a jerk of the harness, off they went, racing through the sky.

"Ho, ho, ho!"

laughed Santa.

"We'll soon have these presents delivered to the Aloha State!"

Santa's sleigh flew through the starry night, heading south across the Arctic Ocean. On they flew in the crisp, wintry air, crossing over Alaska. In the wink of an eye, the sleigh was flying above the Pacific Ocean. The youngest reindeer was very excited. He had never been away from the North Pole before.

They were just nearing Mt. Ka'ala
when, suddenly, they ran into a thick fog.
Mist swirled around the sleigh.

They couldn't see a thing!

The youngest reindeer was getting a bit worried,
but Santa didn't seem concerned.

"In two miles..."

said the Santa-nav in a bossy lady's voice,

"...keep left at the next star."

"But, ma'am," Santa blustered, "I can't see any stars in all this fog!"
Soon they were

hopelessly lost!

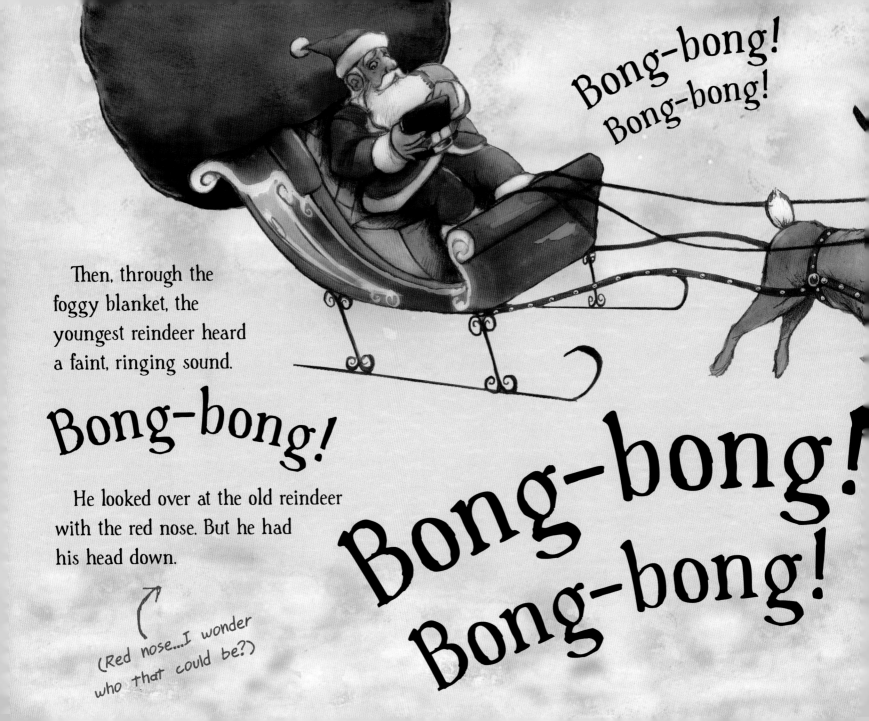

Bong-bong!
Bong-bong!

Then, through the foggy blanket, the youngest reindeer heard a faint, ringing sound.

Bong-bong!

He looked over at the old reindeer with the red nose. But he had his head down.

(Red nose...I wonder who that could be?)

Bong-bong!
Bong-bong!

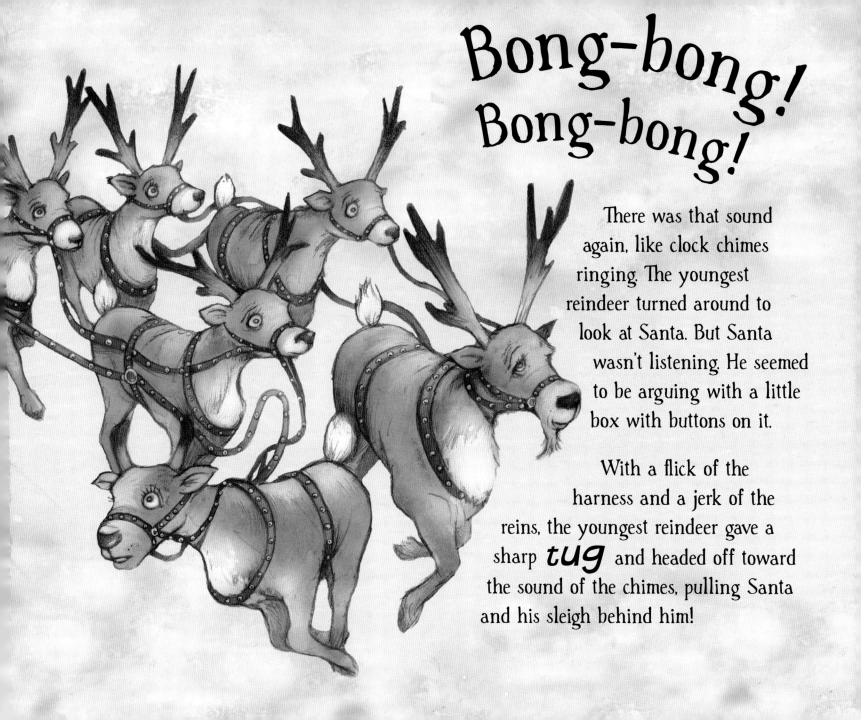

Bong-bong! Bong-bong!

There was that sound again, like clock chimes ringing. The youngest reindeer turned around to look at Santa. But Santa wasn't listening. He seemed to be arguing with a little box with buttons on it.

With a flick of the harness and a jerk of the reins, the youngest reindeer gave a sharp *tug* and headed off toward the sound of the chimes, pulling Santa and his sleigh behind him!

"Whoa!

cried Santa, pulling his hat straight. "What's going on?" Then, to his surprise, he heard the ringing sound.

"Well done, young reindeer!" he shouted cheerfully, "It must be Aloha Tower in Honolulu. Don't worry, children, Santa is coming!"

Then, suddenly...

CRUNCH!

The sleigh hit something as it plummeted through the fog.

"You have arrived!"

said the Santa-nav unhelpfully.

Finally, when the fog had lifted, Santa
discovered exactly where they were...

...stuck, right at the very top
of the Christmas tree near the
Foster Botanic Garden!

"Everybody,
PULL!"

The reindeer *pulled* with all their might until, at last, with a screeching noise, the sleigh scraped clear of the Christmas tree and Santa steered them safely along Interstate H-1, past the National Memorial Cemetery of the Pacific, over the Historic District, and down into Ala Moana Park.

Luckily, there was no
real damage done, but
the packages had all been
jumbled up. Santa quickly sorted
the presents into order again.

"All right," said Santa. "Thanks to this
young reindeer I know where we are
now. Don't worry, children,

Santa is coming!"

Santa drove his sleigh expertly from rooftop to rooftop all over Hawaii, popping in and out of chimneys as fast as he could go.

(Which was pretty fast for a chubby fellow!)

There were big chimneys in Hilo, and small chimneys in Kailua. He squeezed down thin chimneys in Waipahu and plummeted down fat chimneys in Lahaina.

The youngest reindeer was amazed at how quickly they went. Santa never seemed to get tired at all! And it looked like the children in Hawaii were going to be very lucky this year! But the youngest reindeer was starting to feel a bit weary and quite hungry too!

He piled them under the Christmas trees
and carefully filled up the stockings
with surprises.

In house after house, Santa delved
inside his sack for packages of
every shape and size.

Santa took a little bite out of each cookie, a tiny sip of milk, wiped his beard, and popped the carrots into his sack.

In house after house, the good children of Hawaii had left out a plate of cookies, a small glass of milk and, a big, crunchy carrot.

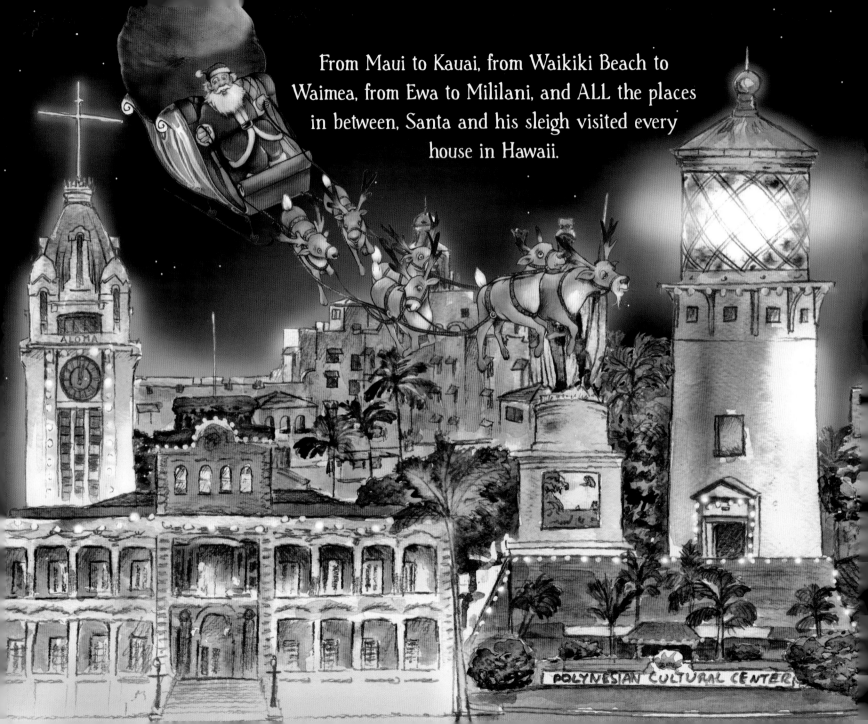

From Maui to Kauai, from Waikiki Beach to Waimea, from Ewa to Mililani, and ALL the places in between, Santa and his sleigh visited every house in Hawaii.

Finally, Santa had delivered the
last present on his long Hawaii list.

"Great moons and stars!" sighed
Santa. "It's past midnight and my sack seems as
heavy as ever! I hope I haven't forgotten anyone."

Santa opened his sack to check...but it was full
of juicy, crunchy carrots!

Santa divided the carrots among all the reindeer.
"Well, done!" he said, patting the youngest reindeer gently on the nose.

But the youngest reindeer didn't hear him...
he was too busy munching!

Then it was time to set off for home. Santa reset his Santa-nav
once more to the North Pole, and soon they were speeding over
Mauna Loa, above Pearl Harbor, and out over the North Shore
through the crisp, starry night.

"Ho, ho, ho!" laughed Santa.

"Merry Christmas, Hawaii!"